G

Gary Grasshopper

Written by Connie Amarel
Illustrated by Swapan Debnath

ISBN 978-1-936352-22-7
        1-936352-22-2

Published by Mirror Publishing
Milwaukee, WI 53214

Printed in the USA.

This book is dedicated to my family and friends, especially those living far away but always close by in my thoughts and in my heart. It is also dedicated to a dear family friend, Gary Gail, who inspired the title character. And last, but not least, to my husband and children, whom I love with all my heart.

Gary Grasshopper wasn't any ordinary grasshopper. He held the record for hopping higher than any other grasshopper in the valley.

He also was known as the happiest grasshopper in the valley and some thought this was the reason why he could hop so high.

But Gary Grasshopper was very sad today. His best friend, Freddie Firefly, had moved to a new valley far away. And no matter how hard Gary tried, he couldn't make his legs hop. He tried over and over again, but he was just too sad to hop.

His other friends, Ivan Inchworm (Freddie called him "Inchy") and Buster Beetle, came to visit Gary and when they saw he couldn't hop, they became very worried about him.

So they thought about it and decided to try to find a way to make Gary happy so his legs would hop again. They knew if they could talk to Betty Butterfly, she would know just what to do.

They sat and talked with Gary and told him of their plan to talk to Betty. Another friend who had stopped by to visit, Tommy Termite, said he would be happy to stay with Gary and try to cheer him up while Inchy and Buster were away trying to find Betty.

So Inchy and Buster left right away. On and on they traveled until soon they came to the dry creek bed where they saw Suzy Snail sunning on a rock. They told Suzy about Gary not being able to hop and asked her if she had seen Betty.

Suzy said that she had seen Betty earlier that day and thought she might be in the rose garden. Inchy and Buster hugged Suzy and told her thanks, then left to go to the rose garden.

They went as fast as they could possibly go until finally they spotted the rose garden up ahead. When they got there and looked around, they couldn't find Betty anywhere. They spotted Lisa Ladybug resting on some fallen rose petals.

They told Lisa about Gary not being able to hop and that they were trying to find Betty to ask for advice. Lisa told them that Betty had left to go to a field far away.

Betty went there to help a firefly who couldn't light up because he was sad about moving away from his best friend. Lisa told Inchy and Buster that the firefly was named Freddie. She remembered that Betty said she would be back later that afternoon.

Inchy and Buster decided to wait for Betty to come back. They stayed in the rose garden until late afternoon but Betty still had not returned. They decided they better go back to Gary's before it started getting dark.

They had just reached the edge of the rose garden, when Lisa called out to them to wait because she could see Betty flying into the rose garden.

They were so happy to finally get to talk to Betty. They told her about Gary being too sad to hop because his friend, Freddie Firefly, had moved away. They asked Betty what they could do to help Gary hop again. Betty smiled as she listened to what they had to say.

She told them she would be glad to go and see if she could help Gary feel better by telling him the same thing she told Freddie. She hugged Lisa and told her she would be back in the morning.

They all waved goodbye as they quickly headed back to see Gary. On the way Betty told them about the new field Freddie had moved to. The way she described it made it sound like a wonderful place for Freddie to live.

When they finally arrived at Gary's house, Tommy was so happy to see them. He told them that even though he spent the whole afternoon trying to cheer Gary up, he was very sad and still couldn't hop.

Betty talked to Gary and told him all about Freddie and how he couldn't light up because he was so sad about moving away from Gary.

Gary was surprised to hear that Freddie was also sad and missed him so much that he couldn't light up. Betty explained that even when a friend moves far away, as long as you think about that friend and keep him or her in your heart, they will never be too far as they will always be close by in your thoughts.

She told Gary that she was sure Freddie
was thinking about him right now, too.
Gary told Betty he would always think
about Freddie and would never forget him.

Suddenly he remembered he had a picture of Freddie in his desk drawer. He told Betty he wanted to put this picture in a very special place.

Betty, Buster, Inchy and Tommy couldn't help but smile when they saw Gary hop over to the desk to get Freddie's picture. They all hugged each other and hugged Gary, who was so happy he could hop again!

Gary placed Freddie's picture next to his bed where he could see him the first thing in the morning and just before falling asleep. He hoped that someday he might see Freddie in person, but until then his best friend would always be only a thought away.

The End

x

CPSIA information can be obtained
at www.ICGtesting.com
Printed in the USA
LVIW010342050912
297404LV00002B